WHISPERS IN THE TWILIGHT

SNEHA SREEKUMAR

Made with ♥ on the Notion Press Platform
www.notionpress.com

My Dearest Family,

In the lottery of life, I hit the jackpot with you. To be able to call you mine is a blessing that fills every corner of my soul with gratitude. This book is a tiny universe we've created together, a place where our dreams and laughter echo in every word. Those early days, when my pen was shaky and my ideas uncertain, your cheers and encouragement were the magic that transformed my doubts into stories. Each step of this journey, with all its twists and turns, has been illuminated by the light of your presence and love.

You've done so much more than believe in my writing—you've breathed life into it. With you, the solitary path of a writer has been transformed into an odyssey of shared dreams and ceaseless support. Every time I thought 'I can't', you were there to gently remind me 'You already have'. You've lifted me from the depths of despair to the heights of joy, time and again.

This book, then, is not just a collection of pages and words—it's a mosaic of our collective soul. It's a testament to your unconditional love, infinite patience, and your uncanny ability to make the impossible seem within reach. As you turn these pages, may you feel the warmth of our laughter, the unbreakable strength of our bond, and the depth of my endless gratitude.

Here's to us—the most incredible team. As we embark on this new adventure, let's carry with us the love and joy that has always been our foundation.

You are the heart of my world, and this book is a small token of my immense gratitude, a thank you whispered from the deepest corners of my writer's heart, with every beat resonating with love and thanks.

Thank you so much for being a part of my story.

Forever Yours,

Sneha Sreekumar

Contents

Introduction

In the heart of Bangalore, where the old meets the new in a dance of timeless rhythm, lies a tale that weaves together the threads of mystery, passion, and the complexities of the human soul. "Whispers in the Twilight" is not merely a novel; it is a canvas where emotions are painted in vivid strokes, and each character is a mirror reflecting the myriad facets of human nature.

Arjun Singh, a senior police officer revered for his dedication and sagacity, stands at the twilight of his career and life. The onset of Alzheimer's is his fiercest battle yet, a fight against the fading of his own memories and identity. His journey is one of courage and vulnerability, of holding onto the fragments of his past while navigating the uncertainties of the future.

Priya Sharma, a forensic expert par excellence, is the embodiment of resolve and intuition. Her brilliance in the field is only matched by the depth of her unspoken emotions. In Arjun, she finds a mentor, a friend, and an unacknowledged love that quietly weaves its way through her heart.

As they delve into the labyrinth of a complex criminal mind known only as The Phantom, Arjun and Priya's paths intertwine in ways they never anticipated. What starts as a professional partnership evolves into a journey of emotional awakening, confronting them with questions of morality, loyalty, and the essence of love.

INTRODUCTION

"Whispers in the Twilight" is more than a crime novel. It is an exploration of the fragility of the human mind, the strength found in companionship, and the unyielding power of love in its most unadorned form. It is a story that promises to take you on a rollercoaster of emotions, from the adrenaline rush of the chase to the heart-wrenching pangs of unspoken affection.

As you turn the pages of this novel, prepare to be transported into the lives of Arjun and Priya, and to become a part of a story that celebrates the resilience of the human spirit. This is a tale that aims to touch your heart and linger in your memory, a whisper in the twilight that resonates with the depths of human experience.

Welcome to "Whispers in the Twilight," a story where every emotion, every twist, and every turn is a step into the depths of the human heart.

Preface

In the hushed moments that linger between night and day, the story of "Whispers in the Twilight" comes alive—a tale not just of mystery and intrigue but of profound human emotions and the indomitable strength of the spirit.

At its core are Arjun and Priya, two souls brought together in the shadowy realms of crime-solving, their paths intertwined by fate and circumstance. Arjun, a seasoned police officer, battles against the encroaching fog of Alzheimer's, a struggle that threatens to dim the brilliance of his storied career. Alongside him stands Priya, a forensic expert whose sharp intellect and quiet resilience mask a wellspring of unspoken feelings.

Together, they are drawn into a web of perplexing crimes, each more mysterious and complex than the last. In their quest to unravel the enigmatic identity of The Phantom, a sinister figure lurking in the darkness, they navigate through a maze of danger and deception. But it's not just the pursuit of justice that binds them; it's a deep, unacknowledged bond of love and mutual respect that grows stronger with every challenge they face.

"Whispers in the Twilight" is more than a mere suspenseful narrative; it is a poignant exploration of the human heart. It delves into the silent battles we fight within ourselves—the yearning for connection, the pain of unrequited love, and the courage to face our deepest fears. As Arjun confronts the shadows of his illness, and Priya grapples with the weight of her unvoiced emotions, their story becomes a testament to the resilience of love in the face of adversity.

This novel invites you to lose yourself in a world where emotions run deep, where the lines between right and wrong blur, and where every whispered secret is a thread in the fabric of a larger, more heart-wrenching narrative. It is a journey that promises to captivate your heart, stir your soul, and leave an indelible mark on your spirit.

As you turn these pages, prepare to embark on an emotional odyssey that intertwines suspense with raw, human emotion. "Whispers in the Twilight" is not just a book to be read; it's an experience to be felt, a journey to be lived, where every word whispers a deeper truth about love, sacrifice, and the enduring strength of the human heart.

Hoping that this story resonates within your heart!

Prologue

Under the kaleidoscopic skies of Bangalore, where the neon lights of tech parks juxtapose the timeless silhouettes of ancient temples, a mystery began to unfold, one that would entangle the city in a web of secrecy and intrigue.

It was an unusually cold night for Bangalore. The city, a pulsating hub of technology and traditional Indian culture, was alive with its usual nighttime fervor. However, in the shadows of its bustling streets, a sinister drama was taking place. In a narrow alley beside a modern high-rise, a body was found. It lay crumpled and lifeless, partly shrouded by the darkness, a stark contrast to the nearby glow of the city's vibrant nightlife.

The victim was a well-known tech entrepreneur, revered in the community for his contributions to Bangalore's booming IT sector. His death was not just a loss to the city; it hinted at a darker turn in the undercurrents of its progress. The initial examination suggested no struggle, no immediate signs of violence. It was as if he had simply laid down and given up his last breath. But the most peculiar aspect was the ancient Sanskrit symbol etched delicately onto his forehead, a symbol associated with Bangalore's rich cultural heritage, but rarely seen in the modern whirlwind of the city.

The crime scene quickly drew the attention of the city's top law enforcement officers, including Senior

Officer Arjun, known for his keen investigative mind and profound understanding of the city's dichotomy. With the initial sweep of the crime scene, Arjun felt the tendrils of something far greater than a simple murder. There was a message here, a silent scream that echoed through the alleyways of the city, resonating with a frequency that only he seemed to pick up.

Forensic expert Priya was also brought in, her reputation for meticulous detail and relentless pursuit of truth preceding her. As she surveyed the scene, her eyes lingered on the symbol on the victim's forehead. It was an anachronism that baffled her, a piece of the past that had inexplicably intruded into the present.

The alleyway, now a crime scene, was a convergence of Bangalore's two souls. On one side, the gleaming glass facade of a tech giant stood proudly, a symbol of the city's rapid technological advancement and global presence. On the other, the weathered walls of an old temple whispered tales of a time when the city was a bastion of culture and spirituality.

As Arjun and Priya delved deeper into the investigation, they found themselves being pulled into the depths of a conspiracy that seemed to intertwine the city's burgeoning tech scene with forgotten lore. The murder was not an isolated incident; it was a harbinger of a deeper malaise that had begun to infect the city. The victim's connections to both the tech world and traditional cultural groups suggested a motive that blurred the lines between progress and tradition, modernity and antiquity.

PROLOGUE

The night air was heavy with secrets, and the city of Bangalore, with its dichotomous soul, stood as a silent witness to the unraveling mystery. In the days to come, the city would reveal its hidden layers, and Arjun and Priya would find themselves navigating a maze that challenged their perceptions of reality and myth, a journey that would test their resolve and shake the foundations of their beliefs.

CHAPTER 1

Guardian of the City's Heart

Amidst the bustling streets and towering skyscrapers of Bangalore, stood Senior Police Officer Arjun Singh. At 35, Arjun was the epitome of what many in the force aspired to be. Tall and athletic, his presence commanded attention whenever he entered a room. His hair, mostly jet black with streaks of silver at the temples, added a distinguished air to his appearance. Deep-set, dark brown eyes, often mistaken for black, mirrored a life dedicated to unraveling mysteries and seeking justice.

Arjun's journey to the police force was a tale of destiny entwined with personal ambition. Born into a middle-class family in a quiet Bangalore neighborhood, where discipline and respect for societal norms were deeply ingrained, he grew up in the shadows of his grandfather's legacy, a revered police officer known for his bravery and integrity. His parents' home was adorned with medals and commendations, a constant reminder of the noble path of service. While his peers dreamt of lucrative careers in Bangalore's booming tech industry, Arjun found his calling in the stories of valor and justice that had captivated him since childhood.

Every morning, Arjun's day began with a jog through the streets of Bangalore, where ancient temples stood alongside modern office buildings, a testament to the city's blend of tradition and modernity. Returning home, he would prepare a simple breakfast, often accompanied by classical Indian music, a nod to his cultural heritage. His home, much like him, was orderly, functional, and devoid of unnecessary embellishments, except for a shelf of dog-eared crime novels, his guilty pleasure.

Arjun's daily routine at the police station was a mix of paperwork, team meetings, and fieldwork. The station, a microcosm of the city's diversity, buzzed with activity. Arjun was known for his approachability, often seen discussing cases with his juniors or sharing a cup of chai with the staff. His desk, amidst the chaos, was an island of meticulous organization.

His relationship with his colleagues was a tapestry of respect, camaraderie, and occasional friction, particularly with his superior, Deputy Commissioner Mehta, whose traditional approach often clashed with Arjun's innovative methods. Yet, it was this dynamic environment that honed Arjun's skills, turning him into an exceptional officer.

Arjun's reputation as a brilliant investigator came from his ability to delve into the psychology of crime. He approached each case with a blend of intuition and methodical analysis, often drawing on his extensive training in criminal psychology and forensic science. His most challenging case to date involved a series of intricate burglaries in high-end Bangalore neighborhoods, which he solved by meticulously piecing together seemingly unrelated clues.

However, Arjun's life was not without its struggles. He was haunted by a growing concern over his moments of forgetfulness - a misplaced file or a forgotten name. These lapses, which he meticulously concealed, were frightening echoes of his mother's battle with Alzheimer's. He feared following in her footsteps, a path of fading memories and lost connections. He ignored all of it, most often, as he felt he wasn't prepared to accept the condition as yet.

Outside his professional life, Arjun was a solitary figure. His relationships were fleeting, strained under the weight of his job and the walls he built around himself. In moments of solitude, he often reflected on his life and the choices he had made, wondering how long he could maintain the facade of invincibility.

Bangalore, with its contrasting worlds, mirrored his own life - one foot in the world of logic and law, and the other in an impending twilight of uncertainty. He often stayed late at the station, poring over case files and planning strategies with his team. His dedication was a source of inspiration for the younger officers, who saw in him a mentor and a role model.

The streets of Bangalore, with their blend of old-world charm and modern hustle, were a constant in Arjun's life. He found solace in the city's vibrant energy, whether it was the early morning flower vendors setting up their colorful stalls or the late-night food carts selling steaming idlis and spicy chai. These simple pleasures provided him with brief moments of respite from his demanding job.

Arjun's relationship with the city was not just professional but deeply personal. He saw himself as a custodian of its safety and order, often going beyond the call of duty to ensure the well-being of its citizens.His involvement in community outreach programs, especially those aimed at youth empowerment and crime prevention, was a testament to his belief in proactive policing.

However, Arjun's relentless pursuit of justice had its costs. The long hours and the stress of the job began to take a toll on his health. He found it increasingly difficult to maintain his fitness regimen, a cornerstone of his physical and mental well-being. His occasional moments of forgetfulness, which he had so far managed to keep under wraps, were becoming more frequent, a source of growing anxiety. At first, the symptoms were subtle, almost dismissible. It started with forgetfulness over trivial things like misplacing his wallet or forgetting appointments. Arjun, attributing these lapses to the stress and fatigue of his demanding job, paid little attention.

However, as days passed, these occurrences became more frequent and more pronounced. There were moments during his routine patrols when he would stop abruptly, momentarily unsure of his destination or purpose. These streets, which he had navigated countless times, momentarily seemed unfamiliar, sending a ripple of concern through his otherwise composed demeanor.

One particular evening stood out. After a long day, Arjun found himself standing in the middle of a busy street. The usual sounds of the city, the honking of cars, and the distant chatter of people, felt unusually overwhelming. For a moment, he couldn't recall why he was there or where he was headed. This fleeting disorientation, though quickly overcome, was a stark reminder of his vulnerability.

Recognizing these signs, Arjun sought medical advice. The diagnosis confirmed his fears – early stages of Alzheimer's. The doctor explained that while the progression could be managed, it was inevitable. Arjun left the clinic with a heavy heart, the weight of this prognosis bearing down on him. The news was a bitter pill to swallow for someone who had always relied on his mental acuity. It forced him to confront the possibility of a future where he might not be able to serve in the capacity he had always known.

As he grappled with this new reality, Arjun began to reevaluate his life. He started to delegate more responsibilities at work, mentoring younger officers to take up roles that he once single-handedly managed. He also began to focus more on his personal well-being, adopting a healthier lifestyle and engaging in activities that improved his cognitive functions, like learning new languages and solving complex puzzles.

Amidst these changes, Arjun discovered a newfound appreciation for the smaller, often overlooked aspects of life. He started to spend more time with his family, rebuilding bridges that his career had strained. His evenings, once consumed by case files and solitary contemplation, were now filled with family dinners and light-hearted conversations.

Determined to maintain his independence and continue his duties, Arjun began adapting to his new reality. He engaged in cognitive exercises, dedicating time each evening to puzzles and memory games. Physically, he remained active, finding solace in long walks and the discipline of his daily routines.

At work, he started to rely more on written notes and digital reminders. His colleagues noticed the subtle changes – the increased reliance on his notebook, the extra time he took to recall certain details – but attributed it to his meticulous nature.

Despite these measures, there were moments that betrayed his condition. In team meetings, Arjun occasionally found himself struggling to remember key points or losing track of conversations. These instances were rare, but they were a reminder of the challenges he faced.

Arjun's journey with Alzheimer's became an integral part of his life, much like his career in law enforcement. He faced it with the same courage and determination that had defined his years of service. This personal challenge did not diminish his resolve to serve; instead, it added a new dimension to his understanding of strength and resilience.

He took on a more strategic role in the police force, utilizing his experience and insights to guide policy decisions and training programs. He became an advocate for mental health awareness within the force, encouraging his colleagues to take care of their mental well-being as diligently as they did their physical fitness.

As Arjun adapted to this new chapter in his life, he realized that his journey was not just about upholding the law or solving cases. It was about understanding the fragility of the human mind and body, the importance of balance, and the need to be kind to oneself. His story, like the city he loved and served, was one of resilience, adaptation, and the relentless pursuit of a better tomorrow.

As the city moved with its usual chaotic grace, Arjun stood as a testament to the strength and adaptability of the human spirit. His legacy was not just in the cases he solved or the accolades he received, but in the lives he touched, the officers he mentored, and the quiet battles he fought and won, both in the line of duty and within himself.

CHAPTER 2

The Forensic Tapestry

In Bangalore's cityscape, where tradition weaves through the fabric of modernity, Priya Sharma stood as a paradigm of the new age forensic expert. At 22, her presence in the forensic department was as striking as a comet in the night sky. Her persona was a blend of delicate grace and formidable intellect, embodying the spirit of the city she called home.

With her long, raven-black hair often tied back in a no-nonsense bun, Priya's hazel eyes spoke volumes of her keen observation and deep-seated curiosity. Her lithe, agile frame was a testament to a disciplined regimen of yoga and mindfulness, practices rooted in her cultural heritage. These physical attributes, coupled with her sharp intellect, made her a notable figure in the halls of the Bangalore Police Department.

The seeds of Priya's journey into forensic science were sown in her childhood. Raised in a Bangalore suburb by a father who was an engineer and a mother who taught literature, her upbringing was steeped in a culture of academic excellence and insatiable curiosity. The Sharma household buzzed with intellectual discussions, fostering in Priya a love for inquiry and analysis.

From a young age, Priya exhibited a natural aptitude for the sciences. Her analytical mind found joy in the complexities of biology and chemistry, subjects she excelled in during her school years. Academic success was not just an expectation but a norm for her, and she embraced this with a passion that was both rare and admirable.

It was during a high school visit to a local police station that Priya first encountered the fascinating world of forensic science. The experience was transformative; the blend of science and justice ignited in her a fire that would guide her future pursuits. Priya's educational journey led her to the esteemed Indian Institute of Science (IISc), a beacon of higher learning renowned for its rigorous academic programs and groundbreaking research. At IISc, Priya immersed herself in the world of forensic science, a field that perfectly married her love for science and her deep-seated desire for justice.

University life was not without its challenges for Priya. Balancing the demanding coursework with her own high standards of excellence often meant long nights in the laboratory and endless hours poring over textbooks. She sometimes grappled with the pressure of expectations, both self-imposed and from the prestigious environment she was in. The competitive atmosphere of IISc pushed her to her limits, but it also forged in her a resilience and determination that would become cornerstones of her character. It was a whirlwind of learning and discovery. Her natural propensity for science, combined with her relentless work ethic, saw her excel in her studies. The university's laboratories became her second home, a sanctuary where she honed her skills and expanded her knowledge. She was particularly intrigued by the minutiae of forensic work – the way tiny fibers, fingerprints, or traces of chemicals could unfold the stories of untold crimes.

One particular challenge that stood out during her time at IISc was a project on trace evidence analysis, a complex and intricate aspect of forensic science. This project required not only a deep understanding of the subject but also meticulous attention to detail and precision in experimentation. The project pushed Priya to explore the limits of her capabilities and, in doing so, reinforced her passion for forensic science.

Her breakthrough came in her final year, during a national forensic science conference hosted by IISc. Priya presented a paper on advanced DNA analysis techniques, a work that garnered significant attention for its innovative approach and practical implications in solving crimes. This presentation was a pivotal moment in Priya's journey. It caught the eye of key members from the Bangalore Police Department who were in attendance.

Impressed by her expertise and the depth of her research, the Bangalore Police offered her an internship in their forensic department. This opportunity allowed Priya to apply her academic knowledge to real-world scenarios, bridging the gap between theory and practice. Her dedication and skill during the internship were undeniable, and upon graduating with distinction from IISc, she was offered a full-time position in the department.

Joining the forensic department of the Bangalore Police was a dream come true for Priya. It was a chance to make a tangible difference, to use her skills in the pursuit of justice. It was more than a job; it was the realization of a dream, the opportunity to apply her knowledge to real-world scenarios, to bring closure to cases shrouded in mystery. Her journey from the classrooms and laboratories of IISc to the challenging environment of the forensic department was marked by relentless pursuit of knowledge, resilience in the face of challenges, and an unwavering commitment to her field. In this new chapter of her life, Priya was ready to face the complexities of real-world crime solving, armed with her expertise and driven by her passion for justice.

Her introduction to the practical world of forensics was a stark contrast to her academic experiences. Here, science met the gritty reality of crime. Her first day at the department threw her into the deep end – analyzing evidence from a complex crime scene. The weight of responsibility was immense, but so was her resolve to meet the challenges head-on. Her approach to evidence analysis was meticulous, each piece of data scrutinized and interpreted with scientific precision. Her reports were comprehensive, leaving no stone unturned in her quest for the truth. Her findings often played pivotal roles in cracking cases, earning her the respect of her colleagues and superiors alike.

However, the path was not without its obstacles. In a field often dominated by male colleagues, Priya faced skepticism and underestimation. But she faced these challenges with unwavering resolve, letting her work speak for her capabilities. Her professionalism and competence eventually won over even her most skeptical peers.

Away from the rigors of her profession, Priya found solace in the arts and culture of Bangalore. She was an avid reader, her apartment a cozy nook filled with books of all genres. Music, especially classical Indian ragas, was a balm to her soul, connecting her to her cultural roots in a city that was rapidly embracing globalization.

Despite her professional dedication, Priya's personal life was a tapestry of simple pleasures and profound interests. In stark contrast to her high-intensity career, her personal life was a haven of tranquility and introspection.

Living in a modest yet aesthetically pleasing apartment in one of Bangalore's serene neighborhoods, Priya had created a space that was both a reflection of her inner self and a sanctuary from the outside world. Modest yet comfortable, her home was a reflection of her personality – organized, efficient, and adorned with personal touches that spoke of her love for the arts and literature.

The walls were adorned with a mix of traditional Indian art and contemporary paintings, a nod to her love for her cultural heritage and her appreciation for modern creativity. The living room was dominated by a well-stocked bookshelf, housing an eclectic collection ranging from classic literature to modern scientific treatises, revealing the breadth of her intellectual interests.

Priya's love for reading was not just a hobby; it was her gateway to different worlds and ideas. She found solace in the pages of novels, where she explored lives and experiences far removed from her own. Her reading list was as diverse as her personality, spanning genres from intricate mysteries, which she enjoyed deciphering, to profound philosophical works that prompted deep introspection.

Music played a pivotal role in Priya's life. She had a deep-seated love for classical Indian music, especially the intricate ragas that she found both calming and spiritually uplifting. Her mornings often began with the soothing strains of a raga, setting a serene tone for the day. Despite her busy schedule, Priya made time to attend classical music concerts, immersing herself in the rhythmic complexities and the emotional depth of the performances.

Priya's culinary skills were another aspect of her multifaceted personality. Influenced by her mother's traditional cooking and her own explorations of various cuisines, her kitchen was a place of experimentation and joy. She enjoyed hosting small dinner gatherings for her close friends, where she showcased her culinary talents with a range of dishes that were as much a feast for the senses as they were a reflection of her diverse tastes.

Her personal relationships, though few, were deep and meaningful. Priya valued quality over quantity in her friendships, maintaining a close circle of friends who shared her interests and values. These relationships provided her with a support system, offering comfort and understanding in a world that was often demanding and relentless.

In terms of romance, Priya's life was quiet. Her commitment to her career and her introspective nature meant that she had little time for romantic pursuits. She believed in the idea of love but was content with waiting for the right person to come along, someone who would understand and share her passions and dreams.

Physical fitness and mental well-being were also integral to Priya's life. She practiced yoga and meditation regularly, disciplines that helped her maintain her physical agility and mental clarity. These practices were not just routines for her; they were essential components of her lifestyle, helping her manage the stress of her demanding job and keeping her grounded.

Despite her accomplishments and the fast-paced nature of her professional life, Priya's personal life was a testament to her belief in living a balanced and grounded existence. Her home, interests, and relationships were reflections of her multifaceted personality, a blend of traditional values and modern aspirations, embodying the spirit of the city she called home.

As Priya navigated her career in forensic science, her path was destined to cross with Senior Police Officer Arjun Singh. This encounter would not only challenge her professionally but also lead her on a journey of personal discovery, one that would delve into the complex interplay of emotion and duty. In Priya, the Police Department had found not just a forensic expert but a visionary, a young woman whose brilliance was set to redefine the landscape of crime investigation in the city.

CHAPTER 3

First Major Crime Scene

In Bangalore, where the old and the new converge in a symphony of colors and sounds, a crime scene had unfolded, piercing the ordinary rhythm of the city. It was here, in the historically rich and bustling area of Malleswaram, known for its blend of traditional bazaars and modern cafes, that Arjun found himself standing, surveying the scene with the keen eye of experience. The morning sun beat down relentlessly, casting stark shadows that seemed to emphasize the gravity of the situation.

Arjun, a figure of authority and seasoned wisdom in the Bangalore Police Department, stood amidst the hive of activity. His tall stature, accentuated by a posture that spoke of years in the force, made him a prominent figure at the scene. His face, weathered by time and the sun, bore the lines of countless cases, each leaving its own mark on his soul. His eyes, dark and penetrating, scanned the surroundings, absorbing every detail, yet he found his attention momentarily diverted as a new presence entered the scene.

Priya, a forensic expert recently assigned to the department, made her way through the crowd with a sense of purpose. Her arrival shifted the dynamics subtly, as she commanded attention not just for her striking appearance but for the air of professionalism that surrounded her. Her hair, dark as the midnight sky, was pulled back neatly, framing a face that exuded intelligence and focus. Her hazel eyes, sharp and perceptive, scanned the area with analytical precision. She moved with a grace that seemed out of place in the grim setting, her white lab coat a stark contrast against the colorful backdrop of Malleswaram.

Arjun, despite his discipline and focus, found himself momentarily captivated by her youthful beauty. She exuded an aura of vibrant intellect, which he found unexpectedly disarming. For a fleeting moment, he allowed himself to admire her, before a voice within reminded him of the professional boundary that lay between them, and of his personal battle against the encroaching shadows of Alzheimer's.

"Officer Singh?" Priya's voice, resonant with confidence, broke through his reverie. She extended a hand in greeting. "Priya Sharma, forensic expert. I've been briefed on the situation."

Arjun, regaining his composure, shook her hand with a firmness that spoke of his resolve. "Welcome to the scene, Ms. Sharma. Your expertise is crucial here."

Their handshake was brief, yet it was a silent exchange of mutual respect. Priya's grip was firm, her gaze meeting his with a determination that echoed her commitment to her profession.

"Shall we?" Priya gestured towards the cordoned-off area, her demeanor shifting to one of focused professionalism.

As they walked towards the body, Arjun briefed her on the specifics. "The victim is a male, estimated in his forties, found by a local early this morning. No visible signs of a struggle or immediate cause of death. We're treating this as a suspicious death given the circumstances."

Priya listened intently, her eyes meticulously observing the scene. "Was the body moved at all?"

"Only to confirm death. We've kept the scene intact for your analysis," Arjun replied, watching as Priya began her examination with practiced precision.

The body lay in a narrow alleyway, partially shaded by the overhanging balconies of old, time-worn buildings. The victim was dressed in what once might have been a crisp white shirt and khaki trousers, now marred by the unforgiving passage of time and circumstance. His shoes, well-worn but of good quality, hinted at a life of modest means yet careful self-presentation.

Priya knelt beside the body, her hands donned in latex gloves as she began her detailed examination. She noticed the lack of any personal belongings, no wallet, watch, or even a ring - items that one would expect to find on a person. This absence could suggest a robbery, yet there was a peculiar sense of order to the victim's appearance that contradicted the chaos of a violent theft.

Her gaze then turned to the face. The victim's features were relaxed, an unusual expression for someone who might have met an unexpected and possibly violent end. There were no apparent signs of trauma, no bruising, cuts, or abrasions that would indicate a struggle. Priya carefully examined the hands, noting the clean fingernails and the lack of defensive wounds.

The skin bore a slight, almost imperceptible, discoloration, a detail that might have been easily overlooked by an untrained eye. Priya speculated that it could be an indication of poisoning or asphyxiation - causes of death that would leave minimal external signs.

Arjun watched as Priya's attention shifted to the positioning of the body. The way the victim lay, with one arm resting slightly above his head and the other folded across his chest, suggested that he might have been placed post-mortem. This detail, in conjunction with the absence of any signs of a struggle or trauma, strengthened the possibility that the victim's final moments might not have occurred in this alleyway.

As Priya stood up, her mind was already piecing together a narrative, albeit incomplete. "Officer Singh, there are aspects here that don't quite add up," she mused aloud. "The lack of personal effects, the relaxed facial expression, and the positioning of the body. It seems we might be looking at a crime scene that is not the primary location of the incident."

Arjun nodded, his experience in law enforcement affirming her observations. "You think he was brought here after the fact?" he asked.

"It's a strong possibility," Priya replied. "The way he's been laid down almost respectfully... it doesn't align with a random act of violence. We need to consider scenarios where the victim knew his attacker or was caught in a situation that didn't start out violent."

Arjun nodded, his experience telling him that this case was more than a simple open-and-shut. "Your insights are invaluable, Ms. Sharma. This area of Malleswaram is usually quiet at night, not the usual spot for something like this."

Priya stood up, brushing off her hands. "I've always enjoyed puzzles, Officer Singh. Complex they may be, but not unsolvable." As they concluded their initial work at the crime scene, Arjun felt a sense of professional gratitude for Priya's presence. Her youth and intellect brought a fresh perspective to the case, a reminder of the passion he had for his work before his diagnosis of Alzheimer's.

"Thank you, Ms. Sharma," Arjun said as they parted ways, a genuine note of appreciation in his voice. "I await your findings with interest." Priya offered a determined smile. "You'll have them as soon as possible." As the forensic team began to carefully process the scene, Priya's thoughts were already on the autopsy she would conduct. Each piece of evidence was a silent witness to the final chapter of the victim's life, and it was her task to listen and interpret their stories.

Watching her leave, Arjun was left with a mix of emotions. There was a professional admiration for her skill and dedication, tinged with a poignant reminder of the relentless passage of time. In Priya, he saw a bright new flame in the twilight of his own career, a beacon of hope in the complex world of crime and justice in Bangalore.

Arjun regarded Priya with a newfound respect. Her keen observation skills and analytical approach were exactly what this case needed. "I'll have my team canvas the area for any witnesses or surveillance footage. With Malleswaram being such a busy area, there's a chance someone might have seen something."

As he turned back to the scene, Arjun felt a renewed sense of purpose. He would use his experience and knowledge for as long as he could, fighting against the tide of his condition. And in Priya, he saw a worthy partner, a new guardian of justice ready to take up the mantle in the ever-evolving landscape of crime in Bangalore.

The sun climbed higher in the sky, casting a harsh light on the alley, accentuating the surreal nature of the scene. Priya's analytical mind was already racing ahead, contemplating the next steps. "I'll need to conduct a full autopsy to confirm these preliminary observations and possibly identify any toxins or substances that might have contributed to his death. Additionally, a thorough examination of the victim's clothes and any trace evidence we can collect here might yield more clues."

The first meeting between Priya and Arjun had set the stage for a collaboration that would blend experience with scientific acumen. Amidst the maze of its streets and the stories they held, a new chapter in crime-solving had begun, with Priya at its center, ready to unravel the mysteries that lay hidden in the shadows.

CHAPTER 4

Deepening Mystery

The sun hung low over the bustling streets of Malleswaram in Bangalore, casting elongated shadows that merged with the evening lights. The historic neighborhood, a blend of the old and the new, had become the center of a perplexing investigation led by Arjun and Priya. The crime scene, now quiet and deserted, still echoed with the unanswered questions that had brought them together.

The victim, identified as Rajat Gupta, was a middle-aged man with no apparent enemies or criminal connections. His body was found in an alleyway, a place he had no known reason to visit. The lack of struggle at the scene suggested a meeting rather than an ambush, a theory that Priya's forensic analysis supported.

"Rajat's financial records show nothing out of the ordinary, but his phone records are a different story," Arjun mused, sifting through the stack of papers on his desk. The dim light of his office cast a thoughtful glow on his face, highlighting the deep lines of concentration etched on his forehead.

Priya, seated across from him, looked up from her own files. "I noticed that too. Several calls to an unknown number the night before his death. No name attached."

"The phone's location was traced to a high-end area in Indiranagar," Arjun added, connecting the dots. "Far from Rajat's usual haunts in the city."

Their investigation had taken them from the victim's modest apartment in Jayanagar to the glitzy streets of Indiranagar, painting a picture of a man living a double life. Each discovery led to more questions, weaving a complex web that challenged both their professional skills and their growing personal connection.

As the case progressed, late-night discussions at the station became their norm. Over cups of strong, steaming coffee, Arjun and Priya delved into the intricacies of the case, their minds working in tandem to unravel the mystery.

One such night, as they pored over the evidence, Priya's keen eye caught a discrepancy in the autopsy report. "The toxicology report shows traces of a rare poison, one that's not easy to come by. It suggests premeditation, a planned murder."

Arjun leaned forward, his interest piqued. "That narrows our suspect list. We need to find out where this poison could be sourced."

The investigation led them to the darker underbelly of Bangalore, where illicit dealings and high-stakes transactions were the norms. Their search brought them to a clandestine establishment, hidden away in the less frequented parts of the city.

As they stepped into the dimly lit space, Arjun's protective instinct kicked in. He was acutely aware of Priya's presence beside him, her determination matching his own, but the unknown elements of their surroundings put him on high alert.

"We're not exactly welcome here," Priya whispered, her eyes scanning the room.

Arjun nodded, his hand instinctively resting on his service weapon. "Stay close. Let's find what we came for and get out."

Their inquiries led them to a shadowy figure, known only as "The Chemist," a man whose reputation for procuring rare substances was well-known in certain circles. Arjun's interrogation of The Chemist was a delicate dance of veiled threats and promises. Priya watched, her admiration for Arjun's tact and experience growing. Despite the challenges of his Alzheimer's, he navigated the conversation with a skill that spoke of his years in the force.

The information they gleaned was invaluable – The Chemist confirmed selling the poison to an unknown buyer, a transaction that happened days before Rajat's death. The description he provided, though vague, gave them their first real lead. As they left the establishment, the tension of the encounter lingered between them. In the safety of the night air, Priya turned to Arjun, her gaze intense. "That was risky, but necessary. You handled that well."

Arjun, feeling the weight of her gaze, was momentarily lost for words. The proximity of danger had brought a new dimension to their relationship, a realization of how much they had come to rely on each other. “Part of the job,” he finally said, his voice low. “But I’m glad you were there with me.”

Their ride back to the station was filled with a comfortable silence, both lost in their thoughts. The case was evolving, drawing them deeper into a world of secrets and lies. And as they navigated this world, their reliance on each other grew, a bond forged in the fires of their investigation.

Over the following days, Arjun and Priya worked tirelessly, following leads, interviewing potential witnesses, and piecing together the puzzle. Each clue brought them closer to the truth, but it also brought them closer to each other, their professional respect blossoming into something deeper, something neither had anticipated.

The breakthrough came unexpectedly. A witness came forward, a local vendor from Indiranagar, who had seen Rajat on the night of his death. His account led them to a luxurious apartment complex, a place where the city’s elite mingled.

Arjun and Priya, standing at the door of the potential suspect, exchanged a look of mutual understanding. This was it – the moment that could unravel the case. As they knocked on the door, the tension between them was palpable. They were partners, in every sense of the word, united by their quest for justice and an unspoken acknowledgment of the feelings that had grown between them.

The door opened, revealing a new chapter in their investigation, a chapter that would test their skills, their resolve, and the depth of the connection that had formed in the shadows of the case.

CHAPTER 5

Personal Insights

The door to the suspect's apartment in Indiranagar swung open, revealing a world that seemed disconnected from the streets of Bangalore where Arjun and Priya had been gathering clues. They stepped into an opulent setting, the air heavy with the scent of affluence and hidden secrets. The plush interior, adorned with expensive art and lavish furnishings, was a stark contrast to the humble alley of Malleswaram where Rajat Gupta's body was discovered.

The suspect, a man in his early fifties with an air of cultivated sophistication, greeted them with a carefully measured surprise. His eyes, sharp and calculating, flickered with a hint of apprehension as he ushered them into the living room.

"Mr. Vikram Reddy, I presume?" Arjun's voice was calm, but firm, as he introduced himself and Priya. "We have some questions about your association with Rajat Gupta."

Vikram settled into an armchair, his posture relaxed yet alert. "Of course, Officer Singh. I'm happy to help in any way I can," he replied, his tone smooth but tinged with underlying tension.

Priya, standing beside Arjun, observed their host. Her mind, trained to notice the slightest details, cataloged his reactions – the fleeting glances, the slight twitch of his hand, the too-casual crossing of his legs. She interjected, “Mr. Reddy, were you aware that Mr. Gupta was found dead two days ago?”

Vikram’s facade faltered momentarily. “Dead? That’s... that’s shocking news. I had no idea.”

Arjun watched the suspect closely, his experience in interrogation telling him that Vikram was more involved than he let on. “You two were involved in a business venture together, correct? One that didn’t end on good terms.”

As Vikram responded with well-rehearsed ease, Arjun’s mind worked tirelessly, piecing together the verbal and non-verbal cues. But beneath his composed exterior, a battle raged silently. The early stages of Alzheimer’s had begun to erode the sharpness of his mind, a fact he had concealed beneath a façade of routine and meticulous note-taking. In moments like these, where every detail was crucial, the fear of losing his grasp on clarity loomed large.

Priya, attuned to Arjun’s demeanor, sensed a subtle shift in his focus. She took the lead seamlessly, pressing Vikram with questions about his financial dealings and the nature of his disagreement with Rajat.

As the interrogation progressed, Vikram’s initial composure began to crack, revealing glimpses of the man behind the mask. The financial transactions and the soured business deal painted a picture of motive and opportunity.

Leaving Vikram's apartment, Arjun felt a mixture of professional satisfaction and personal apprehension. The case was moving forward, but so was his battle with Alzheimer's.

Back at the station, Arjun found himself alone in his office, the files and evidence spread out before him. The silence of the room was a stark contrast to the chaos of his thoughts. Memories of his early days on the force, the accolades, and the challenges, mingled with the fear of a future marred by the relentless progression of Alzheimer's. The thought of becoming a shadow of the man he once was, of losing the ability to serve and protect, weighed heavily on him.

In the solitude of his office, Arjun allowed himself a moment of vulnerability. The walls he had built, the routines he had established to keep his condition at bay, seemed fragile against the inevitable tide of forgetfulness and confusion that threatened to engulf him.

The next morning, as Arjun and Priya reconvened to discuss the case, the weight of his internal struggle was evident in his demeanor. Priya, perceptive as always, noticed the subtle changes – the brief hesitations, the occasional distant look in his eyes.

"Arjun, is everything alright?" she asked, her voice laced with concern.

Arjun, caught in the unguarded moment, quickly masked his lapse with a practiced ease. "Just a long day. The details of this case are starting to blur together," he replied, steering the conversation back to the task at hand.

Priya seemed to accept his explanation, but her eyes lingered on him a moment longer, filled with unspoken questions and a hint of worry.

As the investigation continued, Arjun found himself relying more on Priya's keen insights and observations. Her presence, her unwavering focus, became a beacon in the fog that threatened to cloud his mind. Unbeknownst to her, she was not just a partner in solving the case but a source of strength in his personal battle against Alzheimer's.

The breakthrough in the case came unexpectedly. A piece of overlooked evidence, a receipt from a high-end store found in Rajat's apartment, provided the missing link. It connected Vikram Reddy to the night of the murder, placing him at the scene with a motive to silence Rajat.

As they pieced together the final elements of the case, Arjun's respect for Priya grew. Her dedication, her ability to connect the dots where others saw only disjointed pieces, was not just impressive; it was inspiring.

The day they finally closed the case, bringing Vikram Reddy to justice, was bittersweet for Arjun. The satisfaction of solving the case was tempered by his awareness of the relentless progression of his condition.

In the quiet of his office, after the paperwork was filed and the accolades given, Arjun sat alone, reflecting on the journey. The case had been a testament to his experience and skill, but it had also been a reminder of his vulnerabilities.

The knock on his office door broke his reverie. Priya stood there, a smile on her face. "We did it, Arjun. Another case closed."

Arjun looked up at her, a mix of gratitude and affection in his eyes. "We did, thanks to you. You've been... more than just a colleague, Priya."

Priya's smile widened, her eyes reflecting a depth of emotion that went beyond professional camaraderie. "And you've been more than just a mentor, Arjun."

As she turned to leave, Arjun knew that the case they had solved together was just one part of their story. The journey they had embarked on was more than a pursuit of justice; it was a journey of mutual respect, of unspoken feelings, and of two people finding strength in each other.

As the city moved on, Arjun and Priya stood at a crossroads. Their professional journey had reached a conclusion, but their personal journey was just beginning. A journey marked by the promise of what could be, despite the challenges and uncertainties that lay ahead.

CHAPTER 6

The Bond Begins

In the midst of Bangalore's ceaseless energy, a quiet understanding was blossoming between Arjun and Priya. Their shared journey through the maze of the Rajat Gupta case had unwittingly steered them into uncharted emotional territories, binding them in a camaraderie that transcended professional boundaries.

Seated across from each other in Arjun's office, surrounded by the familiar trappings of their vocation, their conversations often meandered from the rigors of law enforcement into realms more personal, more intimate. The late afternoon sun spilled into the room, casting a warm glow that seemed to mirror the growing warmth between them.

"Arjun, working on this case with you has been a revelation. Your insight, your dedication... it's inspiring," Priya remarked, her tone laced with a respect that had deepened over time.

Arjun, a man who often kept his emotions guarded, felt a stir of something profound. "Priya, the success of this case is as much your achievement as it is mine. Your analytical skills, your unwavering focus... you've been an incredible asset to the team."

The simplicity of their dialogue belied the undercurrent of emotions that flowed beneath. There was an ease, a comfort in their interactions that neither could deny. Arjun, in particular, found himself increasingly captivated by Priya's presence, her vibrant energy a stark contrast to the shadows that lurked in his own life due to his Alzheimer's.

Their discussions, often extending beyond the confines of office hours, revealed shared interests and beliefs. They spoke of their favorite haunts in Bangalore, of music that stirred their souls, of books that had left an indelible mark. And as they shared these pieces of themselves, the connection that had begun as a spark in the chaos of a crime scene grew into a steady flame.

However, amidst this growing closeness, Arjun grappled with an internal turmoil. The progression of Alzheimer's, a secret he guarded fiercely, cast a pall over his moments of happiness. The fear of a future where he might no longer remember the cases he solved, the people he helped, or the bond he shared with Priya, haunted him.

One evening, as Arjun and Priya left the station, a trivial incident of Arjun's car refusing to start led to an impromptu drive through the city's streets with Priya at the wheel. The confines of the car brought a heightened awareness of their proximity, a tangible tension that neither could ignore.

The casual chatter that filled the car was punctuated by moments of silence, heavy with unspoken thoughts and emotions. Priya's occasional glances, filled with a mix of concern and curiosity, did not go unnoticed by Arjun.

"Arjun, you've seemed distant lately. Is everything okay?" Priya's voice broke through the quiet, her words gentle yet probing.

Arjun's initial instinct was to retreat behind a wall of denial, but the sincerity in Priya's eyes compelled him to share a fragment of his truth. "There are personal challenges I've been dealing with, Priya. Challenges that... make me question the future."

Priya's response was a soft murmur of understanding. "We all have our battles, Arjun. But remember, you're not alone."

The simplicity of her words, the offer of support, struck a chord in Arjun's heart. He realized that in Priya, he had found more than a colleague – he had found a friend, a confidante, someone who brought a sense of normalcy to his turbulent life.

In the days that followed, their bond continued to deepen. They found themselves lingering over cups of coffee, exchanging stories and laughter, finding solace in each other's company. The lines between professional and personal began to blur, giving way to a friendship rich with understanding and unexplored potential.

For Arjun, Priya had become a beacon of hope in the fog of his condition, a reminder of the beauty and goodness in the world. Her vibrant presence, her laughter, her keen intellect – all served to momentarily push back the shadows of his fears.

And for Priya, Arjun had become more than a mentor. He was a man of strength and vulnerability, who had quietly stepped into her life and filled spaces she hadn't known were empty. His wisdom, his quiet support, and the glimpses of his seldom-seen smile had become highlights of her days.

As their investigation into other cases continued, their reliance on each other grew. They were partners in every sense of the word, united by a shared passion for justice and an unspoken acknowledgment of the feelings simmering beneath the surface.

As the city wrapped itself in the cloak of night, Arjun and Priya stood at the threshold of a new chapter in their lives. Their professional journey had woven a tapestry of mutual respect and admiration, and now, the personal journey that lay ahead promised an exploration of emotions and connections that neither had anticipated.

Arjun, facing the uncertainty of his condition, found in Priya a source of joy and a reason to cherish each moment. And Priya, drawn to Arjun's depth of character and resilience, saw in him a reflection of her own aspirations and dreams.

Together, they stood ready to face the challenges and possibilities that lay ahead, their bond a testament to the enduring power of human connection in the face of life's unpredictability.

CHAPTER 7

The Phantom Emerges

In the intricate urban tapestry of Bangalore, where the old coexisted with the new, a nefarious shadow had begun to loom large. This shadow, known only as "The Phantom," had emerged as a sinister enigma, orchestrating a series of crimes that baffled the Bangalore Police Department. Arjun and Priya found themselves entrenched in a complex game of cat and mouse with this elusive adversary.

As they sat in Arjun's dimly lit office, surrounded by files and evidence, the weight of the situation was palpable. "The Phantom," Arjun began, his voice heavy with thought, "isn't just a criminal; he's a mastermind. Each crime scene we've encountered, sophisticated and cryptic, bears his signature. It's as if he's challenging us, mocking the system."

Priya, her eyes scanning the reports, added, "His methods are advanced, always a step ahead. It's like chasing a ghost. The theft at the National Gallery, the server sabotage – they're all intricately connected."

Their investigation had led them to the upcoming high-profile event at one of Bangalore's most opulent hotels. A rumor, a whisper in the criminal underworld, hinted at The Phantom's interest in this event. It was this lead that propelled Arjun and Priya to go undercover, immersing themselves in a world of luxury and danger.

The night of the event, as they mingled with the city's elite, their senses were heightened, their every instinct attuned to the slightest anomaly. Priya's intuition was the first to flare. "Arjun, there's something off about one of the staff members," she whispered, her gaze discreetly following a figure whose movements were slightly out of sync with the rest of the staff.

Their pursuit of this lead, however, turned out to be a deliberate diversion – a classic Phantom tactic to distract from his real target. Splitting up to cover more ground, they scoured the area. It was in the dimly lit corridors of the hotel's service area that Arjun finally came face to face with The Phantom.

The man was unremarkable in appearance, but his eyes held a depth of intelligence and malice. "Officer Singh, Ms. Sharma," he greeted them, his voice chillingly calm. "You've been persistent. But you're too late. My plan is already in motion."

Arjun, maintaining his composure, tried to reason with him. "Why are you doing this? What's your motive?"

The Phantom's laugh was cold, devoid of any humor. "Motive? This city, with its façades of law and order, is ripe for a lesson. I am merely an instrument of chaos, exposing the fragility of your so-called justice."

The standoff was tense, a palpable electricity in the air. It was Priya's quick reflexes and Arjun's experience that ultimately subdued The Phantom, ending his reign of terror. In the aftermath, as they processed The Phantom and unraveled his network, the impact of their success resonated throughout the department. They had not only prevented a potential disaster but had also brought down one of the city's most elusive criminals.

The case, however, had taken a toll on Arjun. The exertion of the night had amplified the symptoms of his Alzheimer's, leaving him grappling with a haze of confusion and fatigue. In the quiet of his office, the reality of his condition loomed larger than ever.

It was during this moment of vulnerability that Priya knocked on his door. "We did it, Arjun. But you don't look well. Are you okay?"

Arjun, looking up at her, felt a wave of affection mixed with a fear of the future. "It's been a long night, Priya. But yes, we did it."

As they left the station, the city's nocturnal pulse a backdrop to their own tumultuous emotions, Arjun knew that the journey ahead would be fraught with challenges, both in his professional life and in navigating the uncharted waters of his relationship with Priya.

Their bond had grown stronger, forged in the heat of their shared experiences. For Arjun, Priya had become a beacon of hope, a source of strength against the encroaching shadows of his condition. For Priya, Arjun had become more than a mentor; he was a companion, a confidante, and perhaps something more.

As they stepped out into the Bangalore night, a call came through on Arjun's phone. It was a new case, one that promised to be as sensitive as it was intriguing. A high-profile political figure had gone missing, and the circumstances were mysterious.

Arjun and Priya exchanged a look of determination. The Phantom may have been apprehended, but their work was far from over. Together, they were ready to face whatever challenges this new case might bring, their partnership a testament to their resilience and the unspoken bond that had grown between them.

Under a sky studded with stars, Arjun and Priya stood on the brink of a new adventure. An adventure that would test their abilities, their relationship, and their resolve to uphold justice in a city of endless possibilities.

CHAPTER 8

Intensifying Romance

The news of the missing political figure, Anand Verma, a prominent and influential leader in Bangalore, sent shockwaves through the city. The situation was delicate, the implications far-reaching. Arjun and Priya, still processing the aftermath of The Phantom's case, found themselves thrust into a vortex of political intrigue and danger.

In the confines of Arjun's office, littered with files and photographs, the air was thick with speculation. "His disappearance is not just a high-profile case; it's a chess piece in a larger game," Arjun mused, his eyes scanning the labyrinth of evidence sprawled before them. "We need to consider every angle, Priya. This is not just about finding Anand Verma; it's about uncovering the forces at play behind his vanishing."

Priya, her analytical mind piecing together the disparate clues, nodded. "The last confirmed sighting was at a political rally in Jayanagar. No distress signals, no apparent threats. It's as if he was plucked from the midst of a crowd, invisible to the hundreds around him."

As they mapped out the timeline of events leading up to Verma's disappearance, a pattern began to emerge, one that intricately wove the political fabric of Bangalore with the shadowy threads of The Phantom's operations. It became increasingly apparent that The Phantom was not merely a criminal mastermind but a puppeteer of political tides, his actions reverberating through the corridors of power.

"The Phantom's influence extends beyond the underworld; it's entrenched in the political arena," Arjun realized, a sense of foreboding settling over him. "He's not just committing crimes; he's shaping the political landscape of our city."

This revelation cast a new light on their investigation, transforming it from a straightforward search-and-rescue mission into a complex web of political and criminal intrigue. The lines between lawful governance and lawless ambition began to blur, revealing a network where political figures, business tycoons, and criminal elements converged.

As they ventured deeper into this maze of deception and power, the stakes escalated. Each piece of evidence they unearthed pointed to a sinister coalition, a syndicate where The Phantom was a key player, orchestrating events from the shadows.

Their late-night discussions in Arjun's office often stretched into the early hours, the city's nocturnal soundtrack a backdrop to their intense deliberations. These sessions, while exhausting, brought them closer, their mutual respect deepening into a bond that transcended professional camaraderie.

"This case... it's like peeling an onion," Priya remarked one evening, her eyes reflecting the fatigue of their relentless pursuit. "Each layer we uncover reveals another, more complex than the last. The Phantom, Anand Verma, the political undercurrents – they're all interconnected in a dance of power and secrecy."

Arjun, feeling the weight of the challenge before them, nodded in agreement. "We're up against a nexus of influence and corruption. Unraveling this will require all our skills and perhaps even test our very principles."

In the midst of this daunting task, their relationship evolved, no longer just colleagues but confidants, partners in a journey that was as much about navigating the treacherous waters of their city's power struggles as it was about exploring the uncharted territories of their personal connection.

One evening, after a long day of investigation, Arjun and Priya found themselves at a small café, a rare moment of respite in their hectic schedule. The café, with its dim lighting and soft music, provided a stark contrast to the chaos of their work.

Sitting across from each other, their conversation drifted from the case to more personal topics. Arjun, usually reserved about his private life, found himself opening up to Priya, sharing anecdotes from his past, his hopes, and his fears.

"Priya, I must admit, this case, and everything we've been through... it's made me reflect on a lot of things.

Life's unpredictability, the choices we make," Arjun said, his voice tinged with a rare openness.

Priya listened, her eyes locked on his. "Arjun, working with you, getting to know you... it's changed me. I've seen strength and vulnerability in you, and it's made me realize..."

Her words trailed off, but the emotion in her eyes spoke volumes. The air between them was charged with an unspoken acknowledgment of the connection they shared.

It was in that quiet café that their relationship took an uncharted turn. A turn that was as much about exploring their feelings as it was about navigating the complexities of their case.

As days turned into weeks, their investigation into Anand Verma's disappearance unearthed layers of political machinations and secrets. Their journey took them from the corridors of power to the shadowy fringes of the city, each clue bringing them closer to the truth, and to each other.

One night, as they worked late in Priya's lab, analyzing evidence, the tension of the case and their burgeoning feelings reached a crescendo. Arjun, overcome by a moment of clarity amidst the fog of his condition, turned to Priya.

"Priya, there's something I need to tell you," he began, his voice steady but filled with emotion. "This journey we're on, it's more than just about the case. You've become someone very important to me."

Priya, her heart racing, met his gaze. "Arjun, I feel the same. These past weeks, working with you, being with you... it's made me realize... I have feelings for you." The admission hung in the air, a confession of something that had been growing between them. In the sterile environment of the lab, amidst the evidence and files, a tender moment unfolded. A moment that marked the beginning of a discreet romance, one that added a layer of complexity to their investigation.

As they continued to unravel the mystery of Anand Verma's disappearance, their discreet romance blossomed. Stolen moments in the midst of chaos, quiet conversations in the shadows of their work, their relationship grew, fuelled by mutual respect and a deepening emotional connection.

However, with the romance came a heightened sense of risk. The nature of their work, the stakes involved in the case, made their relationship a delicate affair. They navigated their feelings with caution, aware of the professional lines they dared not cross openly.

The breakthrough in the case came unexpectedly. A piece of overlooked surveillance footage, a chance sighting at a remote farmhouse on the outskirts of the city, led them to Anand Verma. The rescue was dramatic, fraught with danger and political implications.

In the aftermath, as they ensured Anand Verma's safety and processed the culprits involved, Arjun and Priya found themselves hailed as heroes. But amidst the accolades and the relief, their thoughts were on each other, on the journey they had embarked on together. The case of Anand Verma's disappearance had brought them into a vortex of danger and political intrigue, but it had also solidified their bond. A bond that was as much about the thrill of solving crimes as it was about exploring the unspoken depths of their feelings.

Under the canopy of a star-lit sky, Arjun and Priya found themselves at the epicenter of a case that had gripped the city's consciousness. The disappearance and subsequent rescue of Anand Verma had catapulted them into the limelight, heroes in the public eye, but it was within the quieter confines of their shared experiences that their true story unfolded.

The rescue operation had been nothing short of harrowing. Infiltrating the farmhouse where Anand Verma was held, they had navigated a maze of danger and deception. It was their combined skills – Arjun's seasoned instincts and Priya's sharp intellect – that had ensured success. But as they had worked side by side, under the cloak of danger, the bond between them had solidified, forged in the fires of shared adversity.

In the days that followed, as the city hailed their success, Arjun and Priya grappled with the duality of their situation. Publicly, they were celebrated detectives; privately, they were two individuals navigating the waters of a burgeoning romance, concealed beneath the surface of their professional personas.

Their moments together, once confined to the sphere of investigations and strategy, now took on a different hue. Shared glances across the room, subtle exchanges laden with meaning, the occasional brush of hands that sent ripples of unspoken emotion – these were the small yet significant affirmations of their growing connection.

One evening, as they sat in a quiet corner of a quaint café, away from the prying eyes of the world, they allowed themselves the luxury of being just Arjun and Priya, not the detectives, but two individuals bound by an emotion that was as exhilarating as it was terrifying.

"Priya, I never imagined I'd find someone who understands me the way you do," Arjun confessed, his voice a soft murmur amidst the clink of coffee cups and the low hum of conversation around them. "In this line of work, in the life I've led, it seemed like an impossible thought."

Priya reached across the table, her fingers tentatively brushing against his. "Arjun, being with you, working alongside you... it's opened a world I didn't know existed. There's a fear of the unknown, but there's also this... this undeniable pull." Their conversation meandered through the landscapes of their hearts and minds, a gentle exploration of the emotions that simmered beneath their stoic exteriors. They spoke of hopes, of fears, and of the delicate balance they were trying to maintain between their professional duties and personal feelings.

However, amidst the warmth of their connection, a shadow lingered – the shadow of Arjun's Alzheimer's, a specter that hung over their heads, unspoken but ever-present. Arjun, acutely aware of the progression of his condition, grappled with the fear of a future where he might not be able to remember these moments, where the clarity of his thoughts and emotions might fade into obscurity.

It was this fear that held him back, that made him cautious about fully giving in to his feelings for Priya. He was torn between the joy of their growing closeness and the haunting apprehension of his inevitable decline. Priya, sensitive to the unspoken undercurrents, sensed Arjun's internal struggle. She wanted to reach out, to offer comfort and understanding, but was unsure how to breach the barriers he had erected.

Their journey together, however, was destined to take a turn. A new development in the Anand Verma case brought them back into the whirlwind of their professional responsibilities. A piece of evidence, previously overlooked, had surfaced, pointing to a deeper political conspiracy linked to Anand Verma's disappearance. As they delved back into the case, the complexities of their personal relationship were momentarily set aside, replaced by the familiar rhythm of their investigative work. They found themselves back in Arjun's office, surrounded by files and evidence, their minds attuned to the puzzle that lay before them.

"Looks like we've only scratched the surface of this case," Priya remarked, her eyes scanning the new evidence. "This conspiracy... it goes deeper than we thought. There are powerful forces at play here." Arjun, poring over the files, felt a familiar surge of adrenaline. "We're treading on dangerous ground, Priya. This case could have far-reaching implications. We need to proceed with caution."

Their investigation took them down a rabbit hole of political intrigue and shadowy machinations. They uncovered a network of corruption and power play, with Anand Verma as both a pawn and a participant. Navigating this new terrain required every bit of their collective wit and expertise.

As they worked tirelessly, the case not only brought them face to face with the darker aspects of power and politics but also served as a reminder of the strength of their partnership. In the pursuit of truth, they were a formidable team, their individual strengths complementing each other, their mutual trust a foundation that held strong against the tides of adversity.

However, with each passing day, as they inched closer to unraveling the conspiracy, the unspoken thoughts and emotions that simmered between them grew more insistent. The case, with all its twists and turns, was not just a professional challenge; it was a backdrop against which their personal story was being written.

As the city navigated its own complexities and contradictions, Arjun and Priya found themselves at the epicenter of a storm that was as much personal as it was professional. Their journey together, which had begun in the shadowy aftermath of The Phantom's capture, had evolved into a narrative of mutual respect, deepening affection, and uncharted emotional territories.

As they stood on the brink of a major breakthrough in the case, their eyes locked in a moment of shared understanding, they knew that no matter what the future held, the journey they were on was one of discovery and depth. A journey that was shaping not just the course of their professional lives but the very essence of their personal ones.

In Bangalore, where every street has a story and every shadow a secret, Arjun and Priya were charting a path that was as unpredictable as it was inevitable. Their story, woven into the fabric of the city's ceaseless energy, was a testament to the enduring power of connection, the complexities of the human heart, and the unyielding pursuit of truth and justice.

CHAPTER 9

A Twist in the Tale

In the dimly lit confines of Arjun's office, a storm was brewing. Police Department, still buzzing from The Phantom's capture, was about to be shaken by a revelation that would alter the course of the investigation. Arjun and Priya, deeply entrenched in the Anand Verma conspiracy, faced a turning point when Inspector Mehta entered, his face a canvas of grave concern.

"Arjun, Priya, this is critical," Mehta announced, placing a thick dossier on the desk. "We've uncovered startling information about The Phantom. It changes the entire scope of our investigation."

The dossier revealed a network of crimes, sophisticated and diverse in nature, all leading back to a single point of origin - Vikas Rao. There were meticulously planned heists, manipulations of evidence in high-profile cases, and orchestration of riots that seemed spontaneous but were actually intricately designed. But what struck them most was the revelation of a massive embezzlement scheme that siphoned funds from various government projects into a network of offshore accounts, a scheme that implicated some of the highest-ranking officials in the city.

The breakthrough in the case came when Priya, analyzing patterns in the criminal activities attributed to The Phantom, noticed anomalies in their execution. "These crimes... they bear the signature of someone who knows our procedures inside out," she deduced. "Someone with intimate knowledge of police operations."

Arjun, confronted with this evidence, felt a deep sense of betrayal. Vikas Rao, his mentor, the man who had shaped his career and values, was the criminal mastermind they had been chasing all along. "Vikas... he was always a step ahead because he knew exactly how we would react," Arjun realized, his voice tinged with a mix of anger and sorrow.

As they delved deeper, the motive behind Vikas Rao's descent into criminal masterminding began to unravel. Years ago, Vikas had faced a devastating betrayal by the very system he upheld. A corruption scandal, involving high-ranking officials he had trusted, led to the wrongful death of his daughter, a young lawyer fighting against the system's corruption.

This event shattered Vikas Rao. The grief and anger transformed him, turning his brilliant mind against the system he once served. He became The Phantom, using his intimate knowledge of police operations and criminal networks to orchestrate a series of elaborate crimes. Each act was a strike against the corrupt system, a twisted form of justice for his daughter's untimely death.

"Vikas Rao's actions... they were driven by a personal vendetta," Inspector Mehta revealed, his voice heavy. "He used his position to manipulate both the underworld and the law, all to avenge his daughter."

Arjun, struggling to come to terms with the revelation, felt a deep sense of betrayal. The mentor he revered, the man he had emulated, had become the very embodiment of the lawlessness he fought against. "He was supposed to uphold justice, not take it into his own hands," Arjun murmured, his belief system shaken.

"Vikas... How could he? Why?" he murmured, his voice a mix of disbelief and betrayal. Priya, witnessing Arjun's turmoil, reached out, her hand gently touching his. "Arjun, I'm so sorry. I know how much he meant to you."

Arjun's eyes, usually a wellspring of strength, now reflected a vulnerability Priya had never seen before. "He was more than a mentor, Priya. He was a guiding light in my life. To find out he's The Phantom... it's a betrayal I never saw coming." The discovery personalized the conflict for them in a way they had never anticipated. It brought a new layer of complexity to their investigation and to their relationship. They were no longer just chasing a criminal; they were unraveling a personal tragedy. Arjun found himself at a loss for words. The mentor he had looked up to, the man who had shaped his career, was the architect of the very crimes he had dedicated himself to solving.

Priya, seeing Arjun's turmoil, reached out to him. "Arjun, this... this is not just your battle. We're in this together. We'll bring Vikas to justice for everything he's done." Their resolve was tested as they delved deeper into unraveling Vikas Rao's elaborate scheme. The investigation took them through a labyrinth of deceit and manipulation that spanned years. Vikas had used his knowledge of the police force and his connections to orchestrate a series of crimes that were both a challenge to the system and a smokescreen for his larger plans.

As they pieced together the evidence, the depth of Vikas's betrayal became apparent. He had not only manipulated events but also played on the emotions and trust of those who had looked up to him, including Arjun.

The emotional toll of the revelation on Arjun was profound. The man he had once considered a role model was now the target of his investigation. Every memory, every piece of advice Vikas had given him, was now tainted with the knowledge of his betrayal. Priya stood by Arjun as he navigated this tumultuous journey. Their relationship, strengthened by adversity, became a source of comfort and strength for Arjun. In Priya, he found not just a partner in his professional pursuits but also a confidante in his personal struggle.

Their breakthrough came when they uncovered Vikas's ultimate plan – a scheme that would have caused widespread chaos in Bangalore, a final act of defiance against a system he had grown to despise.

Arjun and Priya, now armed with the full knowledge of Vikas's actions, set out to confront him. They received a lead on Vikas Rao's whereabouts. The operation was fraught with danger and emotional conflict. As they closed in on Vikas's hideout, a nondescript warehouse on the outskirts of the city, the weight of the moment settled on Arjun's shoulders.

The confrontation was tense and emotional. Arjun faced Vikas, the man he had once admired, now the architect of the city's turmoil. "Why, Vikas? Why choose this path of destruction?" Arjun implored, seeking closure.

Vikas, standing amidst the evidence of his crimes, responded with a mixture of remorse and defiance. "The system is broken, Arjun. My daughter's death at the hands of corrupt officials was the last straw. I chose to fight against it in the only way I knew how – from the shadows, using the very knowledge that the system imparted to me."

The capture of Vikas Rao marked the end of a painful chapter for the Police Department. For Arjun, it was a personal ordeal, having to bring down the man who had been his mentor. The victory was marred by the realization that the fight against crime often blurred lines between right and wrong, especially when personal vendettas were involved.

In the aftermath, as the department processed Vikas and unraveled his criminal empire, Arjun and Priya emerged as unlikely heroes. Yet, for Arjun, the triumph was bittersweet. He had stopped a criminal mastermind, but in doing so, he had lost a mentor and a part of himself.

As they walked out of the station, they had faced one of the city's greatest challenges and emerged stronger, both professionally and personally. In a city of endless stories and hidden mysteries, Arjun and Priya had carved out their own tale – a narrative of love and courage, of facing the shadows of the past and embracing the possibilities of the future.

CHAPTER 10

The Vanishing Act

In Bangalore's bustling landscape, a new enigma had presented itself to the city's guardians of law and order. Arjun and Priya were facing a perplexing series of events that had rattled the city's tech sector. Top executives of renowned tech firms were disappearing under mysterious circumstances, only to reappear with a gap in their memories, a puzzle that defied logical explanation.

As they sat in Arjun's office, surrounded by files that held more questions than answers, the gravity of the situation was palpable. "These disappearances, they're methodical, leaving no trace until the individuals resurface. It's as if someone is playing a twisted game," Arjun noted, his expression one of deep concentration.

Priya, her eyes reflecting her analytical mindset, added, "The pattern is too consistent to be coincidental. There's a purpose behind these abductions, a motive we need to uncover."

Their investigation led them into the heart of Bangalore's tech hub, a place pulsating with innovation and ambition. Here, in this nerve center of technological advancement, they began to unravel a web of corporate rivalry, espionage, and deeply personal vendettas.

The deeper they delved into the case, the more entangled they became in its complexities. Long hours spent in the labyrinth of corporate dealings and shadowy tech underworlds blurred the lines between their professional and personal lives, drawing them closer in their shared pursuit of the truth.

One night, the case took a dramatic turn. A confidential informant contacted them with a lead, a clue that promised to shed light on the heart of the mystery. Arjun and Priya found themselves in a dimly lit, nondescript coffee shop, waiting for the informant who could potentially crack the case wide open.

The informant, a nervous, bespectacled individual, slipped into the seat across from them. "The disappearances," he whispered, his voice tinged with fear, "they're not just random. They're targeted, part of a larger scheme orchestrated by someone with a vendetta against the tech giants."

The information was a revelation, a key that unlocked a new realm of possibilities. The informant's data led them to a secluded facility on the outskirts of Bangalore, a place that seemed innocuous from the outside but housed a labyrinth of secrets within.

Arjun and Priya, along with a carefully assembled task force, planned a raid on the facility. The night of the operation, under the cover of darkness, they approached the site, the air thick with tension and anticipation.

The facility, a maze of high-tech security and hidden chambers, was more fortified than they had anticipated. As they navigated the corridors, the sense of impending confrontation grew. It was in the heart of the facility that they encountered the architect of the scheme – a brilliant but disgraced former tech mogul, driven to the edge by corporate betrayal and a thirst for revenge. His plan had been to destabilize the tech sector, to inflict a wound on the industry that had ousted him.

The confrontation with the mogul was a clash of ideologies – his disillusionment and desire for retribution against Arjun and Priya's unwavering commitment to justice. Words were exchanged, a volatile mix of accusation and justification, as they tried to reason with him.

In a tense standoff, with the task force closing in, the mogul attempted a desperate escape. It was a moment of chaos, a flurry of movement that ended with his capture.

As they processed the mogul and unraveled the full extent of his operation, the impact of their success rippled through the department. The case had not only been a professional triumph but also a testament to the strength of Arjun and Priya's partnership.

As the city breathed a sigh of relief, Arjun and Priya found themselves reflecting on the journey they had undertaken. The case had been a labyrinth of secrets and lies, but it had also been a crucible that had forged their bond stronger. "Priya, every case we solve, every challenge we face, it brings me closer to you," Arjun confessed as they stood on the rooftop of the police department, looking out over the city. "You've become my anchor, my guiding star."

Priya, standing beside him, her eyes reflecting the city lights, replied, "And you, Arjun, have become my heart's quiet solace. In this world of chaos and uncertainty, you are my constant."

Their embrace, under the canopy of the night sky, was a silent vow – a promise to face the future together, whatever it might bring.

Their moments together, once stolen in the shadows of their work, now took on a new depth. They found comfort and strength in each other's presence, a respite from the demands of their profession. One evening, as they walked through the serene paths of Cubbon Park, the city's heartbeat a distant echo, they allowed themselves to be just Arjun and Priya, away from the roles they played in their professional lives.

Their walk turned into a quiet conversation, an exchange of thoughts and feelings that had been simmering beneath the surface. It was a moment of vulnerability, of sharing fears and dreams, of acknowledging the deep connection that had grown between them.

As they continued their journey, the bond they shared was no longer just a product of circumstance. It was a choice, a conscious decision to explore the possibilities that lay ahead, together.

CHAPTER 11

Echoes of the Heart

In the vibrant tapestry of Bangalore, a city where every dawn brought new stories, Arjun and Priya found themselves amidst a narrative that was as deeply personal as it was professional. The mystery of the tech moguls' disappearances had been resolved, but it was the mystery of their own hearts that now took center stage.

In the days following the case, their relationship blossomed like a secret garden, hidden away from the world's prying eyes. They were partners in crime-solving by day, and by night, they explored the depths of a romance that had quietly woven itself into the fabric of their lives.

One evening, as they walked through the serene Sankey Tank, the setting sun cast a golden hue over the landscape, mirroring the warmth that radiated between them. Arjun, usually a fortress of strength and composure, found himself in a whirlwind of emotions he had never dared to explore before Priya.

"Priya," he began, his voice a soft cadence amidst the rustling leaves, "these moments with you, they've become the most cherished part of my days. You've brought light into a life I thought was destined for darkness."

Priya, her hand gently resting in his, looked up into his eyes, her own shining with unspoken affection. "Arjun, being with you has been a journey of discovery. You've shown me strengths I didn't know I had, and in you, I've found a love I didn't think was possible."

Their stroll turned into a dance of words and emotions, a gentle ebb and flow of confessions and assurances. They spoke of their fears, their hopes, and the delicate tendrils of love that had entwined their hearts.

As they found a secluded spot, the world around them faded into a blur. In that tranquil haven, they shared their first kiss – a moment that sealed their unspoken promises, a culmination of the longing and affection that had simmered beneath the surface.

In the days that followed, their romance deepened, blossoming into a bond that was as profound as it was private. They shared stolen moments in the midst of their busy lives, each glance, each touch, a testament to the depth of their feelings.

However, amidst the crescendo of their love, a shadow loomed – the secret of Arjun's Alzheimer's. It was a specter that had haunted him, a truth he had kept shrouded, fearing it would taint the purity of what they shared.

One evening, as they sat on the terrace of Priya's apartment, overlooking the cityscape bathed in the glow of twilight, Arjun knew it was time to unveil the veil of his secret.

"Priya, there's something I need to tell you," he began, his voice laced with a hesitancy that was uncharacteristic of him. "Something about me, about my future."

Priya, sensing the gravity of the moment, turned to face him, her expression a blend of concern and attentiveness.

Arjun took a deep breath, the weight of his confession pressing upon him. "I have been diagnosed with early-onset Alzheimer's," he revealed, the words hanging in the air like a delicate yet somber melody.

The revelation hit Priya like a wave, a torrent of emotions crashing over her – shock, fear, and a profound sense of empathy. "Arjun," she whispered, her voice trembling with emotion. "Why didn't you tell me before?"

Arjun, his eyes reflecting the turmoil within, replied, "I was afraid, Priya. Afraid of how it would change things between us, afraid of becoming a burden to you."

Priya reached out, her hands cupping his face, a gesture of tenderness and strength. "Arjun, you could never be a burden. This... this changes nothing about how I feel for you. We'll face this together, every step of the way."

In that moment, as they held each other, the city lights flickering like distant stars, their love transcended the boundaries of mere words and gestures. It became a beacon of hope, a force that bound them together against the uncertainties of the future.

The revelation of Arjun's condition brought a new layer of depth to their relationship. It was no longer just about stolen moments and whispered confessions; it was about standing together in the face of life's most daunting challenges. Under the canopy of stars, on Priya's terrace, the air was thick with a mélange of emotions. Arjun, having revealed his deepest secret, felt a vulnerability he hadn't experienced in years. Priya, her eyes glistening with unshed tears, grappled with the myriad emotions that Arjun's confession had stirred in her.

"Arjun, I wish you had told me sooner," Priya said softly, her voice a tender caress in the cool night air. "We could have faced this together, right from the start."

Arjun looked into her eyes, the usual resolve in his gaze giving way to a gentle earnestness. "I know, Priya. But I was scared... scared of how it might change us. You've brought so much light into my life, I couldn't bear the thought of losing that."

Priya took his hands in hers, their fingers intertwining, a physical manifestation of their emotional bond. "Arjun, love doesn't diminish in the face of challenges. It grows stronger. And my love for you... it's not bound by the fears of what the future holds."

They sat in silence for a moment, the night around them a cocoon of intimacy. The revelation of Arjun's condition had opened a floodgate of emotions, and in its wake, their relationship found a new depth.

"Priya, you've shown me a strength I didn't know I had," Arjun continued, his voice tinged with emotion. "With you, I feel I can face anything, even this."

"And you will, Arjun. We will," Priya affirmed, her tone resolute. "We'll navigate this together. Your battle is mine, just as my heart is yours."

Their conversation meandered through the landscapes of their fears and dreams. They spoke of the challenges ahead, of Arjun's treatment and the support he would need. But more than that, they spoke of their love – a love that had become their anchor in the tumultuous sea of life.

As the evening deepened, they found comfort in shared stories, in laughter and tears, in the gentle caress of hands and the warmth of shared silence. The terrace, bathed in the soft glow of the night, became a sanctuary, a haven where they could be vulnerable and strong in equal measure.

In the days that followed, their bond grew stronger. Priya became Arjun's steadfast partner, not just in their professional endeavors but in his personal journey through the early stages of Alzheimer's. She was there at his doctor's appointments, offering a listening ear and a comforting presence. Arjun, for his part, found in Priya a reason to embrace each day with hope and courage. Her love was a constant reminder of the beauty that still existed in his world, a world that was slowly becoming more challenging to navigate.

Their discreet romance evolved into a profound partnership, one that was tested and tempered by the realities of Arjun's condition. They cherished each moment, knowing that time was a gift not to be taken for granted.

One particularly poignant evening, as they sat by the tranquil waters of Ulsoor Lake, watching the gentle play of light on the water, Arjun spoke of his fears.

"Priya, there's a part of me that's terrified of the day I might not remember you, the love we share," he said, his voice barely above a whisper.

Priya, her heart aching with the weight of his words, leaned closer. "Arjun, you've etched yourself so deeply in my heart that even if a day comes when you don't remember me, I'll remember for both of us. I'll be here, holding on to our love, to the memories we've created."

Her words were a balm to his soul, a promise that transcended the limitations of memory and time. In Priya, Arjun found not just a lover but a guardian of their shared past and an unwavering companion for the future. It was a love built on the foundations of trust, understanding, and an unshakeable bond that grew stronger with each challenge they faced.

CHAPTER 12

In the shadows of tomorrow

Bangalore, a city pulsating with life and energy, was a tapestry of stories, each thread intertwining with the next. In this vibrant setting, Arjun and Priya found themselves at the crossroads of a new challenge, one that tested the strength of their bond and the resilience of their spirits.

A series of bizarre incidents had begun to surface across the city. Unexplained power outages, mysterious cyber attacks, and strange occurrences in the tech district created a sense of unease. The city that thrived on its technological prowess was now being haunted by an invisible adversary.

Arjun and Priya, still navigating the complexities of their relationship in the wake of Arjun's Alzheimer's diagnosis, were called to investigate these anomalies. As they sat in Arjun's office, surrounded by reports and data, the weight of the new case was palpable.

"These incidents, they seem disconnected, but I can't help but feel there's a pattern we're missing," Arjun mused, his brow furrowed in thought.

Priya, her analytical mind piecing together the information, nodded in agreement. “It’s as if someone is testing the city’s vulnerabilities, probing for weaknesses. We need to find the connection.”

Their investigation led them down a labyrinth of leads. They delved into the heart of Bangalore’s tech world, interviewing experts, and chasing down leads. The more they uncovered, the more convoluted the case became, a puzzle that was as perplexing as it was alarming.

Amidst the professional turmoil, their personal lives were a haven of solace. Their relationship, a once-hidden bloom, had flourished into a profound partnership. They found comfort in each other’s presence, strength in shared silence, and joy in brief moments stolen from the demands of their work.

One night, as they worked late in the cyber unit, surrounded by screens and data, the line between professional and personal blurred. The room, bathed in the soft glow of monitors, became a cocoon, isolating them from the world outside.

“Arjun, do you ever think about how different our lives would have been if we hadn’t met?” Priya asked, her voice a whisper in the quiet room.

Arjun turned to her, his eyes reflecting the soft light. “Every day, Priya. And I thank fate every time for bringing you into my life. You’ve become my anchor in this storm.”

Their conversation was a dance of words and emotions, a sharing of fears and hopes. In the sanctity of that room, they allowed themselves to be vulnerable, to lay bare the depth of their feelings.

As the case progressed, they found themselves chasing a shadow, a mastermind who seemed to be always one step ahead. The incidents across the city escalated, each one more daring than the last, culminating in a massive cyber-attack that threatened to cripple Bangalore's tech infrastructure.

The attack was a wake-up call, a realization that they were dealing with an adversary of considerable skill and malice. Arjun and Priya, along with their team, worked tirelessly, their every resource and skill brought to bear on the investigation.

It was during a late-night session, poring over lines of code and patterns of attacks, that Priya made a breakthrough. "Arjun, look at this. The pattern of these attacks, it's familiar. It's similar to a case we worked on years ago."

Arjun leaned in, his mind racing as he examined the data. "You're right, Priya. This isn't just about causing chaos; it's personal. Someone is using their knowledge of the city's systems against us."

Their investigation took a sharp turn, leading them into the realm of old cases and forgotten enemies. The more they unraveled, the clearer it became that they were dealing with a vendetta, a ghost from the past seeking retribution. As they closed in on their suspect, the tension between their professional duties and personal lives intensified. Arjun, battling the advancing symptoms of his Alzheimer's, found himself relying more on Priya, her presence a constant in his increasingly turbulent world.

The conversation that unfolded was a tapestry of emotions and reflections. They spoke of the case, dissecting each decision, each clue, marveling at how intricately their adversary had woven his web of deceit.

Yet, it was the unspoken words, the shared glances, that spoke volumes. In the quiet of the office, with the city's heartbeat a distant echo, they found solace in each other's presence – a solace that had become their sanctuary from the chaos of the world outside.

As they delved deeper into their conversation, the topic inevitably shifted to Arjun's condition. The case had taken a toll on him, the long hours and intense focus exacerbating the symptoms of his Alzheimer's.

"Priya, I won't lie. This case was challenging, not just professionally, but personally. There were moments when I felt the shadows closing in," Arjun confessed, his voice a whisper of vulnerability.

Priya, her hand reaching out to grasp his, offered a smile tinged with both sadness and resolve. "I know, Arjun. But remember, you're not alone in this. We'll face these shadows together, every step of the way."

Their conversation, interspersed with moments of silence, was a delicate dance of emotions – a blend of concern, determination, and an unspoken promise to weather any storm that came their way.

In the following weeks, as they navigated the aftermath of the case and the complexities of Arjun's condition, their relationship evolved. It was no longer just about stolen moments and whispered confessions; it was about being each other's strength in moments of weakness, about finding joy in the simplest of things.

They took to spending evenings together, sometimes walking the bustling streets of Bangalore, other times in the quiet of Priya's apartment, where they could escape the scrutiny of the world. Each moment spent together was a treasure, a memory etched in the canvas of their hearts.

One such evening, as they sat on the balcony of Priya's apartment, watching the sun dip below the horizon, Arjun broached a topic that had been weighing on his mind.

"Priya, there's something I've been thinking about," he started, his gaze fixed on the melting colors of the sky. "I don't know what the future holds for me, for us. But I do know that I want to make the most of the time we have, to create memories that will last, no matter what."

Priya, her heart resonating with his words, leaned in closer. "Arjun, every moment with you is precious. We'll create a lifetime's worth of memories, together." Their conversation that evening was a blend of dreams and plans, of building a future in the face of uncertainty. They spoke of places they wanted to visit, experiences they wanted to share, and the life they envisioned, however unpredictable it might be.

As days turned into weeks, their bond grew stronger. They became each other's confidants, companions in a journey that was as uncertain as it was beautiful. The challenges of Arjun's condition were ever-present, but in Priya, he found resilience and a reason to embrace each day with hope.

Priya, for her part, saw in Arjun a courage and a vulnerability that only deepened her love for him. She admired his determination to live fully, to face the shadows of Alzheimer's with a spirit that refused to be dimmed.

As the city hummed with its customary energy, Arjun and Priya found themselves closing in on the resolution of the puzzling case that had preoccupied them. Their investigation into the unexplained power outages and cyber attacks had taken them through a maze of technological intricacies and corporate espionage.

As they sat in Arjun's office, surrounded by a collage of evidence and reports, Priya pieced together the final elements of the puzzle. "Arjun, look at this," she said, pointing to a pattern in the data. "All the attacks originate from the same source, a rogue element in the tech hub."

Arjun, leaning in to examine the evidence, felt a sense of accomplishment mixed with anticipation. "So, we've found our ghost in the machine. It's time we confronted them."

Their pursuit led them to a clandestine facility hidden within the tech district, a hub of unscrupulous activities masked by a veneer of legitimacy. The raid on the facility was a calculated operation, executed with precision and stealth.

Inside, they uncovered a web of illegal activities – from data theft to sabotage. The mastermind, a disgraced tech wizard with a vendetta against the city's tech giants, was apprehended in a dramatic confrontation.

As the suspect was led away in handcuffs, Arjun and Priya shared a look of triumph. They had unraveled the mystery, restoring order to the city's tech sector and preventing further chaos.

In the aftermath of the case, as they filed their reports and debriefed their team, the weight of their achievement settled upon them. They had not only solved a complex case but had also protected the city they loved.

The evening following the case's closure, Arjun and Priya found themselves at their favorite spot by the serene Ulsoor Lake. The water reflected the hues of the setting sun, mirroring the calm and contentment they felt in each other's presence.

"Priya, this case... it was challenging, but having you by my side made all the difference," Arjun said, his voice laced with sincerity.

Priya smiled, her eyes reflecting the deepening hues of the dusk. “Arjun, we make a great team. Professionally and personally. I can’t imagine going through this without you.”

As they walked along the lake, their conversation meandered through plans and dreams, through the realities of Arjun’s condition, and the strength of their commitment to each other. They spoke of the future with a sense of hope and determination, aware of the challenges but emboldened by their love. The revelation of Arjun’s Alzheimer’s had indeed changed their relationship, but not in the ways they had feared. It had deepened their bond, brought them closer in ways they had never anticipated. In each other, they had found not just love but a partnership that transcended the trials of life. Together, they stepped into tomorrow, their love a guiding light through the shadows of doubt and fear.

CHAPTER 13

The Twilight Melody

Several months had passed in the vibrant city of Bangalore, a city that had witnessed the unfolding of a unique love story between Arjun & Priya. Their relationship, a tapestry of deep affection and shared struggles, faced its most significant challenge yet.

The onset of monsoon had brought with it a reflective mood. Arjun, seated in his office with a view of the rain-drenched city, was lost in thought. The progression of his Alzheimer's had become more pronounced, a shadow that loomed larger with each passing day.

Priya, ever the pillar of support, entered the room with a gentle knock. She found Arjun gazing out the window, a faraway look in his eyes. "Thinking about the case?" she asked, her voice a soothing balm in the quiet room.

Arjun turned, offering a smile that didn't quite reach his eyes. "Not the case, Priya. I was thinking about us. About all the moments we've shared." Priya walked over, taking a seat beside him. She reached for his hand, a gesture of comfort and solidarity. "Arjun, no matter what happens, those memories... they're ours to keep. Forever."

Their conversation, a familiar dance of words and emotions, delved into the heart of their relationship. They reminisced about the cases they had solved, the challenges they had overcome, and the love that had blossomed amidst adversity.

As they spoke, the room filled with echoes of their journey – laughter, tears, and moments of silent understanding. It was a testament to the depth of their bond, a bond that had grown stronger in the face of Arjun's condition.

"Priya, I don't know how much time I have before my memories start to fade," Arjun said, his voice tinged with a poignant mix of fear and acceptance. "But I want you to know, you've been the best part of my life. You've made every moment worth living."

Priya, her eyes brimming with tears, replied, "Arjun, you've been my strength, my guiding light. I'll hold onto our memories, for both of us. And no matter what the future holds, I'll be right here, by your side."

Their conversation was a river of emotions, flowing through the landscapes of their hearts. They spoke of their fears and hopes, of the beauty of their time together, and the cruel twist of fate that threatened to steal it away.

As the monsoon rain continued to pour outside, they made a promise to each other – to cherish each day, to make the most of the time they had, and to face the future with courage and love.

In the weeks that followed, Arjun and Priya continued their work, solving cases and upholding the law. But the shadow of Alzheimer's loomed ever closer, a reminder of the ticking clock on their time together.

One evening, as they sat in the comfort of Priya's apartment, surrounded by the memorabilia of their cases and adventures, they faced a heart-wrenching moment. Arjun, looking at a photograph of them together, struggled to place the memory.

"Priya, when was this taken? I can't seem to remember," he said, his voice a mix of confusion and frustration. Priya, her heart aching at the sight of his struggle, took the photo, her fingers tracing their smiling faces. "It was during the Phantom case, Arjun. One of our first victories together."

Arjun nodded, a sense of loss etching his features. "I'm sorry, Priya. I'm trying to hold on, but it's getting harder."

Priya moved closer, wrapping her arms around him. "It's okay, Arjun. I remember. I'll always remember for both of us."

Their embrace was a cocoon of love and shared sorrow, a moment that captured the essence of their journey.

As time progressed, the moments of forgetfulness became more frequent for Arjun. Yet, in Priya, he found an unwavering support system. She became his anchor, helping him navigate the fog of his fading memories.

They spent their days creating new memories, savoring each moment as if it were their last. Walks in the park, quiet evenings at home, laughter, and tears – each day was a celebration of their love, a defiance of the cruel hand of fate.

But as the inevitable progression of Alzheimer's continued, their moments together became bittersweet. Arjun, aware of his declining condition, grappled with the fear of losing himself, of becoming a stranger to the woman he loved.

One particularly poignant night, as they sat watching the rain from the balcony, Arjun turned to Priya, his eyes reflecting the turmoil within. "Priya, I'm scared. Scared of the day I might not recognize you, of the day I lose myself."

Priya, tears streaming down her face, held his hand tightly. "Arjun, you've given me a love that I'll carry in my heart forever. No disease, no memory loss can ever take that away. I'll be here, Arjun, loving you, even if you can't remember me."

Their conversation that night was a testament to the power of their love – a love that transcended the barriers of memory and time. They vowed to face each day as it came, to find joy in the present, and to keep the flame of their love burning bright, even in the darkest of times.

In the months that followed, as Arjun's condition worsened, Priya stood by him, a beacon of hope and love. She became his memory, reminding him of the life they had shared, of the love that had defined them.

The final chapter of their story was as emotionally charged as it was poignant. Arjun, in the advanced stages of Alzheimer's, was a shadow of the man he once was. Yet, in his lucid moments, in the clarity that occasionally broke through the fog, his love for Priya shone through, undiminished by the ravages of the disease.

Priya, ever devoted, cherished these moments, holding onto them as treasures in the fading light of their shared life. She cared for Arjun with a tenderness and strength that was the hallmark of their love.

In the end, as Arjun lay in the quiet of their home, his journey drawing to a close, Priya was by his side, holding his hand, whispering words of love and gratitude for the life they had shared.

"Arjun, you'll always be in my heart. Our love, our story, it will live on, forever," she whispered, her voice a soft melody in the stillness of the room.

Arjun, in a moment of clarity, turned to her, a faint smile on his lips. "Priya, my love, my life... thank you."

As he slipped away, his final breath a gentle sigh, Priya held him close, her tears a silent tribute to the man she loved, to the story they had written together.

As the city moved on, the tale of Arjun & Priya remained – a story of enduring love, of a bond that transcended the trials of life and the finality of death.

Their love was a beacon of hope, a testament to the strength of the human heart in the face of life's greatest challenges.

Their story, etched in the annals of the city's narrative, was a melody of love and loss, a symphony of emotions that echoed in the hearts of those who knew them. Arjun and Priya's journey, a poignant reminder of the power of love, continued to inspire, long after the final notes had faded into the echoes of the heart.

Epilogue

Months had passed since the city of Bangalore bid farewell to Senior Officer Arjun Singh. The monsoon rains had given way to clear skies, and the bustling streets carried on, as they always do, with the relentless rhythm of life. Yet, in the heart of the city, in the lives touched by Arjun and Priya, a profound narrative of love and resilience continued to resonate.

In the corridors of the Police Department, Priya emerged as an emblem of silent strength and a source of ceaseless inspiration. Her resolve, forged in the fires of shared tribulations and deep love with Arjun, became not just a beacon for her colleagues but also a testament to her own inner fortitude. In her eyes shone the depth of wisdom and understanding, a clear reflection of the emotional and professional odyssey she had embarked upon.

Her moments of solitude were often spent by the tranquil banks of Ulsoor Lake, a place that held countless memories of her and Arjun – their shared laughter, dreams, and contemplative silences. It was here, amidst the gentle caress of the breeze and the soothing rhythm of the water, that she felt Arjun's presence most vividly, as if he was right there with her, sharing the quiet beauty of the lake.

Priya took it upon herself to keep the story of their love and struggles alive. She became a vocal advocate for Alzheimer's awareness, sharing their journey at various events, offering support and understanding to those facing similar battles. Each word she spoke, each story she shared, was imbued with Arjun's enduring spirit, serving as a beacon of hope and a symbol of everlasting love.

The Police Department honored Arjun's memory with an annual award that celebrated the virtues he had embodied – courage, integrity, and compassion. Each year, as Priya presented this award, her speech was not just a formal tribute but a heartfelt remembrance of the man whose life had touched and inspired so many. Her eloquence in these moments provided comfort and healing to those who remembered and still felt his absence.

In the solitude of her apartment, surrounded by photographs that captured their shared journey, Priya found a quiet refuge. Flipping through the albums, each photograph was a window to a cherished memory, a moment frozen in time. Tears mingled with smiles as she remembered Arjun's laughter, his insights, and the deep love they had shared, each memory a precious keepsake of their time together.

The story of Arjun and Priya, though culminating in a bittersweet farewell, had become a beacon of inspiration and hope. It was a narrative that spoke eloquently of the power of love to transcend the trials of life and the inevitability of parting. Their journey, a poignant testament to the resilience of the human spirit, offered comfort and courage to all who heard it.

Within the bustling life of the Bangalore Police Department, and in the vibrant rhythm of the city they both loved and served, the legacy of Arjun and Priya endured. Their tale, a resonant melody of enduring love and commitment, continued to inspire and uplift the hearts of those who knew them, a beautiful reminder that even in the face of life's most daunting adversities, the power of love remains the most formidable and enduring force.

As Bangalore moved forward, the story of Arjun and Priya persisted, not merely as a narrative of loss, but as an ode to an undying love. Their enduring saga, a symbol of hope and resilience, continued to kindle inspiration long after its final chapter was written.

In the timeless echoes of their love, their story lived on—profound and enduring, a celebration of two souls who, amidst life's myriad challenges, found and cherished each other, their love a perpetual flame in the tapestry of life !!!

www.ingramcontent.com/pod-product-compliance
Lightning Source LLC
LaVergne TN
LVHW091118150826
845673LV00002B/879

* 9 7 9 8 8 9 2 3 3 8 0 7 3 *